Graphic design and illustrations: Zapp

Story adaptation: Jane Brierley

© 1996 Tormont Publications Inc.
  338 Saint Antoine St. East
  Montreal, Canada H2Y 1A3
  Tel. (514) 954-1441
  Fax (514) 954-5086

Printed in China

THE UGLY DUCKLING

TORMONT

It was a golden afternoon in late summer. Near a big old house in the country, a mother duck had made her nest by the water.

"These eggs are taking a long time to hatch!" she sighed. She was lonely sitting there all by herself. The other ducks were too busy swimming around to come and chat with her.

At last the ducklings began to peck their way out of the eggs. Their little beaks banged away against the shell. One by one, still wet from the egg, they tumbled onto the floor of the nest. Soon, they stood up and shook themselves until their soft downy feathers became dry and fluffy.

The little ducklings stared with wonder. "How big the world is!" they chirped — and so it seemed, after being inside an egg.

"Oh, the world's much bigger than this," quacked the mother duck. "Now, is everyone hatched? Oh dear, no — that big egg is still there!"

An old duck swam by and stopped to look.
"That must be a turkey egg," she said. "I had
one in my nest once. What a worry it was! The
chick wouldn't go near the water however
much I tried to push it. Just leave it alone, that's
my advice." And she swam slowly away.

"All the same, I'll sit on it a bit longer," the
mother duck thought to herself.

Before long, the mother duck heard a tap! tap! and soon the new baby toppled out of the egg. "Chirp! Chirp!" it cried.

The mother stared. "It certainly isn't a turkey," she thought, noticing the webbed feet, "but it's awfully big and ugly. Well, I'll just have to make the best of it."

The next day, the mother duck led her family into the water. Splash! In went the first duckling. One by one they disappeared under the surface and bobbed up again like little balloons. Soon all of them, even the ugly duckling, were gliding over the water.

The mother then took her family to the
barnyard. "Bow to the old duck," she said. "The
ribbon around her foot means that no one wants
to get rid of her, and that's a great honor."
The ducklings bowed, too much in
awe to even chirp.
The turkey marched up to look
them over. "I've never seen such a big,
ugly duckling!" he gobbled.

That was the beginning of the duckling's troubles. Everyone was mean to him because he was so ugly. The other ducklings bit him and the hens pecked him. The poor duckling was heartbroken.

As time went by it got worse. Everyone seemed to hate the poor duckling because he looked different. His brothers and sisters called him names, and his mother would sigh and say, "I do wish you were somewhere else." Even the woman who fed the poultry tried to kick him.

The ugly duckling couldn't stand it any longer. He ran out of the barnyard and flew over the garden hedge, almost tripping over the top branches. He frightened the sparrows in the hedge, and they flew away as he landed on the other side.

"I'm so ugly that I even frighten the little birds," he thought.

He ran on, as fast as his big, webbed feet would go. Soon he was in the woods, and it became harder and harder to find his way. But he kept on running until he could go no further. He found himself beside a great marsh where wild ducks lived. There he lay, hidden under a bush, feeling very lonely and tired.

In the morning, some wild ducks flew by
and stopped to look at the new arrival.

"Hello," they said. "Who are you?"

"I'm a farm duck," said the ugly duckling.
He stared at the wild ducks, who looked very
different from those in the barnyard.

"A duck?" they squawked. "We've never seen a clumsy grey duckling like you! But we don't mind, as long as you don't marry into our family."

Of course, the ugly duckling didn't dream of marrying anybody. All he wanted to do was to rest by the marsh, far away from the cruel animals on the farm.

19

There was a chill in the air. The ugly duckling noticed that the trees were turning gold and red. As he poked among the reeds for food, two young wild geese landed beside him.

"Hi there, friend!" they called. "Would you like some company? We're flying to another marsh a little farther along, where there are lots of young geese like us." And up they flew once more.

The ugly duckling was happy to follow. But before he could move, a shot rang out. To his horror, the geese fell into the marsh, and a huge dog splashed into the water to fetch them.

Guns began firing all around the marsh. Another dog came trotting through the reeds and almost stepped on the ugly duckling. It looked at him for a moment, then ran away.

"Thank goodness!" gasped the duckling. "I'm so ugly even the dogs don't want me."

He lay perfectly still in the reeds the whole day long. Finally, as the sun began to set, the dogs disappeared and the firing stopped. The duckling scrambled onto the shore and hurried away through the woods.

The wind was blowing very hard as he stumbled along in the dark. Suddenly, he found himself standing in front of a tumbledown old cottage.

A faint light was shining through holes in the door. "I must get out of this wind," thought the duckling. So he scrambled through a hole and huddled in a corner for the night.

An old woman lived in the cottage with her cat and hen.

"And who's this?" she asked the next morning, when she discovered the duckling. "Perhaps you'll give me some duck's eggs, eh?"

The duckling was allowed to stay. The cat and the hen tried to reassure him, "Just lay eggs and learn to purr, and you'll be fine."

But the poor duckling could do none of these things, so he sat sadly in a corner, remembering the joy of gliding over the water. At last he said to the hen, "I want to go into the wide world."

"You're crazy," said the hen, "but I won't stop you."

The duckling managed to find a big pond, and there he floated in the sunshine, day after day. Once, a flock of great white birds with long, graceful necks flew by. He had never seen such beautiful birds. "If only I could be their friend!" he thought.

The cold winter winds began to blow. The duckling had to paddle hard to keep ice from forming. One morning, his feet froze into the ice among the reeds.

A passing farmer saved him. He took the poor bird back to his warm home. But later, the farmer's children frightened the duckling. He flapped about the kitchen, knocking things over, and when the door opened for a moment, out he flew!

Somehow, the duckling survived the winter. One morning, as he lay among the reeds, he noticed how strong the sun felt.

He stretched his wings and flew up into the warm air. Before he knew it, he was flying towards a garden with a big pond in the middle.

There he saw three beautiful white birds gliding gracefully about. They were swans, although he didn't know it.

"I'll join them," he thought. "Perhaps they'll kill me because I'm so ugly, but I'd rather die that way than be pecked by hens."

He glided over to the swans and bowed his head — and there, reflected in the water, was another beautiful swan!

"Look, there's a new one!" cried two little children who had run into the garden. "It's the prettiest one of them all!"

The swan, no longer an ugly duckling, lifted his graceful neck. How delighted he was! His heart filled with love for the other swans, and at last he knew true happiness.